MW01144764

## Praise *for A COLLECTION OF TINY STORIES, Diminutive Tales from the Tip of My Imagination*

*CK Sobey's new book* A Collection of Tiny Stories, Diminutive Tales from the Tip of My Imagination *is an excellent work that can help writers of all abilities who want to further develop their individual styles and improve their creative abilities. To help develop her own imagination, CK focuses on a momentary thought and expands it in a similar fashion that a songwriter would in writing a song. It begins with a key word or phrase that develops into a short glimpse of the subject's "world." Composers call that "the hook." I trust that you will find inspiration in* A Collection of Tiny Stories. Diminutive Tales from the Tip of My Imagination *by CK Sobey and give yourself permission to let the tiny tales forming in your mind find the light of day on a printed page. All of the tiny stories Kas has set into this book have the potential to become books of their own.*

Michael R. Hathaway, DCH—hypnotist, author, musician
White Mountain Reflection Center
Madison, New Hampshire

*Reading CK Sobey's* A Collection of Tiny Stories, Diminutive Tales from the Tip of My Imagination *is like having an open-ended ticket to visit multiple worlds. Each "tiny story" is a postcard from an unseen world. These stories roll back the fog that so often obscures our dreams and our waking imaginations. The art that compliments each story is beautiful and evocative and adds to the experience of the stories. Sobeys tales hold hints of the supernatural, ephemeral visions and colorful fragments that embody the whole of an experience, a relationship, a place. I was unable to put this book down until I finished it!*

Judith Prest, Poet, Artist, Teacher, and Creativity Coach
Author of *Elemental Connections, After* and *Geography of Loss.*
judith@spiritwindstudio.net
www. spiritwindstudio.net

*CK Sobey brings tiny stories that open big doors of imagination and send us sparks to ignite our own creative fires. These stories cover a gamut of life experiences, including wonder, curiosity, illness and death, tenderheartedness, and laughter. The weaving in of images provides visual inspiration that makes this collection even more delightful.*

Gail Warner, MA, MFT, author of *Weaving Myself Awake: Voicing the Sacred through Poetry*, therapist, and
Founder of Pine Manor Retreat Center.

*"The magic is coming back" says the typewriter. Kassia reminds us that it has never left the crevices between moments and invites us to look. These stories are like wild strawberries found while we are walking in the woods on a hot day. You will savor, you will giggle, you will wonder, and sometimes you might shed a tear. The beautifully curated images are poems in themselves. Lose yourself in them and use them as portals to your own imagination.*

Mariabruna Sirabella, MS, LMFT, SCF&T<br>
*www.mariabruna.com*<br>
Founder of the School Of The Origins SoulCollage® Lead Trainer;<br>
Trainings and Translations Coordinator

*This treasure of tiny tales offers tender vignettes carefully crafted with vivid and engaging detail. Entering these imaginary realms, you will find a magical gathering of stories infused with texture, symbolism, and meaning. Surprises around every corner, rich with whimsy, mystery, and longing, brought alive by a masterful storyteller.*

Christina MacLeod, MAEd, MPH,<br>
Creative Healing Alternatives and Holistic Medicine<br>
Nature-inspired Ceremonial Celebrant<br>
www.christinamacleod.com

*CK Sobey has taken the written wanderings of her imagination and gathered them into this delightful,* Collection of Tiny Stories *with big impact. From the sweet to the sorrowful, these magical moments may be real or imagined. Kas seems to ask, if imagined, are they any less real?*

*These stories and exquisite original images will spark the reader's own imagination as they follow Kas's adventures of the mind.*

Patty Kline-Capaldo<br>
Co-founder, Creative Light Factory<br>
www.creativelightfactory.org

A Collection of Tiny Stories *is a whimsical and philosophical collection. With a celebratory tribute to creative spirit, imagination, and daydreaming, there is something for everyone to find and cherish in this gorgeous little book. Relax, read one story at a time, and savor it. The stories and art create a sense of peace and hope that every day can bring moments and memories both pure and poignant.*

Michelle Miller
Executive Director, International
Women's Writing Guild
IWWG.org

A Collection of Tiny Stories, Diminutive Tales from the Tip of My Imagination *presents prose and art that represent an inspirational celebration of the spirit, gathering "tiny" works "born out of moments of whimsy, mystery, and longing." Add "and magic" to that list, because CK Sobey's works employ a magical element that gathers tales both fantastic and reflective into three sections:* Inspiring Odysseys, From the Heart, and Fanciful.

*These short works don't require linear reading. Readers can skip through the sections and will find them succinct, standalone pieces that delight no matter their arrangement or the wellsprings of their wonder.*

*Take* "The Bookstore" *for one example. Here, Sobey reflects that* "I always love going to the bookstore. I go when I'm drained, or my inner animal needs its fur stroked." *The piece goes on to explore the magic of a particular used book that calls his name with intrigue to provide passages that fuel his days:* "I knew we would eventually meet. It was handwritten in a beautiful, fluid script. Intrigue and enchantment came over me. I touched those written words with my fingers, stroking the words."

*The conclusion is a thought-provoking book image presented in full color that lingers in the mind, reinforcing the magic of books.*

"The Art Class" *is another blend of autobiography and reflection that muses on Sobeys participation in a portrait class, and the memories of the past that are reflected in this present-day endeavor:* "I have come to love that younger me more through the years, realizing I had just received a gift from this memory."

*While many of these short pieces hold the look of poetry one-liners, in fact, these vignettes are presented using a minimum of words and an attention to making every one count. The color illustrations that accompany them are simply gorgeous in their own right, accenting the story and creating visual embellishments of their own artistic high quality.*

*Think Proust, but without the prolific descriptions of scenes that thwarted some of his readers. In effect,* A Collection of Tiny Stories *is an exploration of in-the-moment experiences that, like Proust, connect past and present with a simple touch, taste, observation, or experience.*

*Readers who want the feel of a journey through life via its smallest moments that hold the time-traveling power to connect past and present will find* A Collection of Tiny Stories *more accessible than most short collections. It makes the most of the short form to demonstrate the power of the moment and the art in capturing and preserving it and will prove an especially useful selection for literature libraries and teachers looking for contemporary examples of rich prose reflections.*

D. Donovan, Sr., Reviewer,
Midwest Book Review

A COLLECTION OF

# Tiny Stories

*Diminutive Tales from the Tip of My Imagination*

CK SOBEY

A COLLECTION OF

# Tiny Stories

*Diminutive Tales from the Tip of My Imagination*

*Prose and Visual Images*

CK SOBEY

INNER HARVESTING

A Collection of Tiny Stories
Diminutive Tales from the Tip of My Imagination

v2.0

This is a work of fiction. Names, characters, businesses, places, events, locales, and incidents are either the products of the author's imagination or used in a fictitious manner. Any resemblance to actual persons, living or dead, or actual events is purely coincidental.

The opinions expressed in this manuscript are solely the opinions of the author and do not represent the opinions or thoughts of the publisher. The author has represented and warranted full ownership and/or legal right to publish all the materials in this book.



Inner Harvesting

Paperback ISBN: 978-1-7375061-2-6
Hardback ISBN: 978-1-7375061-4-0



PRINTED IN THE UNITED STATES OF AMERICA

This book is for everyone who feels a sense
of the creative spirit rambling around.
She is waiting to share some delight with you.

I also dedicate this book to Beth Moulton.
I had just started to know you.
I will think of you often.

# Foreword

*"In the Universe, there are things that are known, and things that are unknown, and in-between them, there are doors."*

*William Blake*

*The creative spirit is unique in what she offers us. It begins with receiving. It never ceases to amaze me how differently this gift expresses itself in people. This spirit is always waiting to be realized. There are no boundaries. Creativity can be spontaneous. The ideas, the call of inventiveness. It is all (and awe), inspiring, and if I open my arms to accept this imaginative muse, it becomes a lovely, frolicsome, and maddening relationship. Not without effort, but fulfilling.*
*It may inspire to create something of a culinary nature. A recipe that pops into my head or exploring something artful. Maybe dance and the movement teases me with an idea.*
*Strumming a guitar, make some music, tap a rhythm, compose a song!*
*What can you envision with that patch of dirt in front of where you live? Take a trip to visit a garden center with an idea as your partner and plan what you plant in that patch of dirt.*
*Volunteer to be of service. Be silly! Have some fun! If we are lucky, we'll catch the joy and begin a ritual. Maybe give birth to a bunch of little idea babies.*
*The creative process moves in limitless ways. It may stick around for only moments as a mischievous sprite, tempting us to take part, or hang out longer.*
*Accept it. It is a gift that is being given.*
*A few muses hang around me most days. Sometimes it feels like a rabbit that hops along, inviting me to follow down that proverbial rabbit hole. It is a process that I trust, at least to begin. If I am in the flow, the zone, it leads to the next step.*

*The well-known author Elizabeth Gilbert says this of an idea, "Ideas are driven by a single impulse: to be made manifest. And the only way an idea can be made manifest in our world is through collaboration with a human partner. It is only through a human's efforts that an idea can be escorted out of the ether and into the realm of the actual."*
*Ideas are the stuff exquisite greatness is made up of. A waking dream is an idea. Regardless of how large, small, or insignificant, it leads to another stage of an idea. I honor daydreaming.*
*This collection of* Tiny Stories *is an assortment of tiny, brief stories that were born out of moments of whimsy, mystery, and longing. Everyday people I heard about or read about sparked something within me. Many of the stories are from my own life and exploits.*

*I believe in the indefatigable powers of imagination. I do my best to widen my imaginative lens of what I can create in any genre, recipe, or solution to a problem. The list goes on and on. It is what gets me out of bed in the morning. What will the day bring?*
*Not every day is an explosive revelation, with my muses rambling around, whispering to me of some plan. I do my best to find peace and calm, even in moments. When I find these moments, they are the sweetness between the flow of found ideas. The quiet space is what I need to receive. I honor this time to allow the ideas to take shape, to grow.*
*I love pictures as well. They have their own story to tell. As prompts I become turned on to a story, musing, or something new coming all together. I hope you enjoy my visual stories as well. They were created for these stories.*

*I arranged the book into three sections:*
Inspiring Odysseys. *These lean more toward the fantastic, sci-fi, and almost believable.*
From the Heart *is just that. I hope they touch yours.*
Fanciful *entries are whimsical, lighter, and captivating.*

*Read this book in any order, day or night.*
*Find a quiet space and let yourself journey with me to the tip of my imagination. Let your dreams take flight!*

CK Sobey
Valley Forge, Pennsylvania
Winter 2022

# Contents



## Inspiring Odysseys

## From the Heart

## Fanciful

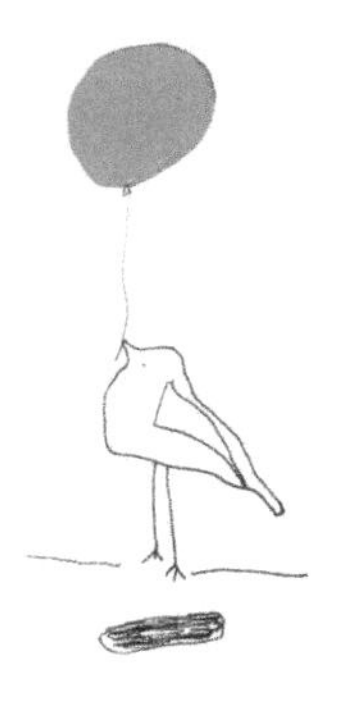

"The next morning when the sun was in the sky,
the river discovered something beautiful.
She saw the blue sky for the first time.
She had never noticed it before."

Thich Nhat Hanh

# My Typewriter

Years ago I bought a typewriter on the internet. The ribbons also came with the typewriter, with directions on how to maintain it. It had a rhythm to it. I loved striking the keys, the sound of the bell when I was at the end of a page, moving the arm over so the typewriter would move down to the next line to type on. I loved the ink on my fingers when I fixed the ribbon or the keys when they stuck.

As time moved forward and technology created newer and better toys, my typewriter became obsolete.

The word processor was next. I could feel the rhythm, the sounds, the inner movement. Even so, it was nothing like the dings and clip-clop patter of my typewriter.

Currently I have my laptop. I still can't find what I had with my typewriter, so I have an app that mimics the sounds of a typewriter. The magic is coming back.

Visual prompts are huge for me. They encourage and stir my creative mind.

I dig deeper to find what's on the tip of my imagination. What opens the door to wild abandonment?

When providence visits, I feel the magic moving down through my fingertips.

The sound of my typewriter comes alive.

I am in the zone.

And the rhythm begins, again!

# Inspiring Odysseys

# A Moment Held

Yesterday I remembered something that happened to me when I was much younger. It forever changed my life.
One night I was looking at the moon and stars.
The night sky was crystal clear. I felt I was in the center of the universe, moonbeams and starlight all around me.
I heard a hum. Not sure where it had come from, I looked around and found a small object. It was a rough stone that glittered.
I brought it home with me.
I wrapped it with care in a scarf and hid the bundled stone behind some books on a shelf.
Then I forgot about it.
Years passed, and life came and went in its multi-complex ways.
Relationships began and ended. I became employed at different jobs, some odd and interesting. I started a few businesses.
Life moved along.
I worked on mastering the art of cooking. I did and became a part owner in a small restaurant.
One day I was searching for a certain book and found that old scarf I had hidden years earlier.
The old scarf was covered with dust.
I opened it that night when the moon was full. I was excited and also anxious about what it might reveal after all this time.
Evening arrived, the moon's precious magic once again shining all her light.

I ate dinner thinking about the stone wrapped in my scarf after all these years. I rinsed my plate and took my folded scarf out to the meadow behind my house.
With hurried hands I untied the small bundle.
I sat for quite a long time under the moonlight, gazing at the once-rough clump of stone. It was smooth.
The same lights still shimmered from somewhere within. I held it in my hand, this magical gift I had found long ago. I sat in the meadow.
Just me, the rock, and the Universe.
I felt I was part of something huge and grand. Comfort bathed me into a deep, relaxed place.

I have never been the same since then and will remember that night my whole life.

I left the stone in the meadow to be found by someone else one day. Now as my eyes close for sleep, I hold the scarf that once held my stone and remember again the enchantment of it all.

# The Amusement Park

It's very quiet here.
I remember the days when children screamed with delight, giggling and chasing each other behind the rides and tents.
Pink cotton candy rose a mile high, kids dunked for crisp apples or bit into the caramel covered ones.
I worked in the big tent. I was a trapeze performer; that was when I was alive a hundred years ago, it seems, and probably was.
Boys in knickers pulled little girls' pigtails. The constant ruckus. The life of it all!
This had been no ordinary amusement park.
This was the largest in the country, traveling from state to state, setting up, then dismantling the rides, the arcades and then putting it all back together in new towns with children's delight, standing by and watching.
That was a life worth living.
I married the Ferris wheel operator, Stan, the love of my life.
We called it the "go-round," back then.
The day the go-round broke down, terrified screams could be heard all over the park.
No one moved. We watched in horror as the children rocked the seats.
Stan shouted my name. I came running as one child tried to scramble out of the top chair.
A woman beside me grabbed my hand. It scared her to death. Silent words murmuring from her quivering lips.
I realized she was praying.
I climbed up the support beams. Behind me other trapeze and high-wire performers followed.
We had worked together for so many years that we instinctively became a team.
I yelled at the kids not to rock. I shouted at the kid climbing out, "Get back in your seat right now," my voice commanding, pleading. He obeyed. I reached for the next bar and then the next, positioning my feet on the support bars.
OK, I thought. I can lift them down one by one to Gloria, to Kurt, and then Stan will grab them. It took hours of slow movement, speaking

quietly to the frightened kids.
We did it!
What a night that was after we closed. We built up a huge bonfire and enjoyed delicious food arranged by our chefs from all over the world. Some homemade beer and some exotic blends added joviality to our celebration.
Strong brewed coffee in the morning.
Next day the town mayor presented all of us with citations. We were very proud.
The amusement park traveled and operated for five more years.
There was another machinery breakdown on the Ferris wheel years later.
We saved the kids again.
I slipped at the last, and that was that. I died.
Such is life. You never know how it's going to happen.

Thanks to our fortune-teller, I chatted with Stan for years until he passed.
Now we don't need the fortune-teller.

# The Babysitter

My mother was at the age when she was sharing stories of her youth. She was in her nineties and still kept her memory. One evening as the family was all sitting around the dinner table just talking about their days, she spoke about a time in her life when she was a very young girl and babysitting.

"I was happy to be spending time again with the twins. They were easy to babysit for. I had known the Petersons forever. They had always been our neighbors.

"I enjoyed my time at their home. It was always an easy few hours of babysitting. They paid me well. My parents were friends with them. We lived a few houses down. It was easy for me to walk over. Mr. Peterson would always drive me home when it was dark," she continued.

I could see my mother seeing it as she told the story.

"There was something disturbing about him, though. When my parents talked about their life, Mr. Peterson would just sit and smile, sharing no stories about his life. He said it would bore everyone, that it had been dull and uneventful. At least that's what Mom told me when I asked about Mr. Peterson."

"Mr. Peterson has nothing he wants to share, dear."

"The last time I was at his house babysitting, I looked around while the twins napped. I had never been in their attic and wanted to know what theirs looked like."

I looked around the table at the others listening, wrapped up in my mother's story.

"My mother had made a playroom in our attic. Upstairs it was boiling hot and dusty. The Petersons had done nothing with the attic. It was stifling and smelled old. I found some old photos in a box. The photos were dry and curled from the heat. I was careful not to crack them. I was nervous and uncomfortable. One picture showed a young man

with another fellow. The other guy had a funny little mustache. He was holding out a stiff arm.

"The other man had his arm around the man with the mustache. Probably good friends. There were many other pictures just tossed in a corner in the attic. The pictures looked like an old movie. There seemed to be hundreds of people lying all over each other. Now that I think of it, I thought they had to be dummies made to look like people. Maybe even thousands. Yes, this was a movie set, I thought then.

"The last picture I could make out was a bunch of men standing around smiling. They all wore uniforms. They were holding their arms out. Maybe some Boy Scout or army thing. Yes, probably a movie. I guess Mr. Peterson's family were actors long ago. I wondered what they called the movie.

"I thought about telling my mother what I found out about Mr. Peterson, but she would get upset and punish me. I decided it was better to keep this secret.

"I was very young then and didn't know the world of monsters."

## A Practice in Perspectives

My clock on the wall has a face that is old and weathered.
It says Coteaux de Loire. In the background on the face, it has a sketch of a winery with farm-like buildings. Again, the face appears old.
I often just look at it and listen to the ticking of my clock on the wall. It has become a mystical, quiet ritual.
The numbers are Roman numerals and the hands on my clock are the kind I have seen on a metronome, delicately made, precise, and sharp like arrows.
The edging all around the face has the look of something that had burned but was caught in time.
Interesting phrase, caught in time.
The soft ticking reminds me of a kitten curling up to a heartbeat. I watch the hands move on a graceful curve. Then in one minute, the smaller of the two lands on the number III, the other on XII.

“I have been on several walls, in many rooms, many places.
You have wrapped me lovingly, carefully placing me in boxes countless years, remembering to remove my batteries so I could sleep in darkness. I then awakened while being placed on a new wall, a new home for us.
I am like a guardian to you. I am aware that now and then you just listen to my heartbeat.”

My relationship with my clock on the wall is a kind of love and blessing.
It has grown deeper over the years.
There are never any disputes or interludes of passionate display.
My clock on the wall is always dependable and pleasing to look at. It never disrupts my concentration or focus.
It is a quiet serenade that keeps me in my zone.
I cannot imagine a more perfect silent partner. I have been aware of this fact since the day I discovered my clock.
It is like finding a kitten just a few days old that needs a beating heart, except I am the kitten and my clock on the wall is always beating for me.

# The Bookstore

The day I walked into the bookstore, I felt something tingling in my belly.

I always love going to the bookstore.

I go when I'm drained or my inner animal needs its fur stroked.

What better place than a used bookstore?

The smells, the dust, the unknown histories of each book.

Just to reach for one that signals me is always a mystical experience.

Who held it last? How many lives had the book touched?

This time, it was different.

In this bookstore there is a section where library books have been marked "withdrawn." In this section, I always find a book to buy for a small price.

One day I went to the bookstore to browse for a book that would interest me. Something strange happened that day.

The *book* and I met on a shelf in the back.

It was a crisp, snowy day outside. The sun was streaming in at angles through the blinds. Silhouettes of light bounced along the walls. Dust particles swirled in free expression. I sat down to read my book in a big, comfortable chair. On the inside page of the book was written: "I knew we would eventually meet."

It was handwritten in a beautiful, fluid script. Intrigue and enchantment came over me. I touched those written words with my fingers, stroking the words, wondering who had written this and when.

I bought the book. Reading the handwritten line has become a ritual for me.

Imagined vignettes come alive. I have begun talking with the book daily. It answers any questions I have.

I don't know where the wisdom comes from.  I just trust.

I begin and end my days with it.

ALSKADE BARN
ATAN

# The Jump

This was it, I thought, as I stared at the view from the top of the ridge.
I waited to jump.
I was number twenty out of twenty-five people designated to soar into the boundless depths of space from a platform suspended in space.
As I watched I breathed deeply as they trained me to wear the oxygen helmet.
This helmet and my space suit would be my entire home for the next several hours.
I exhaled and remembered my home as a boy, the moment before my dad jumped and something ripped away his cord.
While the jumper falls toward earth, the attached line is like an umbilical cord feeding air to the jumper.
Jumping has evolved over the past twenty-five years.
Now jetpacks propel the jumper forward at a greater speed.
No cords remain in use, just the jumper and the graceful, distinct movements each performs during the slow descent.
During the jump we travel through a black, airless void of time and space.
Millions of stars, worlds, and galaxies shine brilliant fragments of lights and colors.
I needed to experience the real thing. I longed for it. To feel the sensation of gliding toward my landing.
I had been training for this day most of my life.
I remember being home with my mother the day they came to tell us about my father.
That nightmare years ago.
That day would shape the rest of my life.
I would follow in my dad's footsteps of being a jumper.
I knew he would be proud of me.
After Dad died, home was hollow.
Mom seemed to quit living for a while.
My grandmother told me my mother was grieving, a natural part of healing.
Now I will carry out this jump for my father.
Wrapped and sheltered in my suit and helmet,
I will make this jump for him in the silence of space.
I won't spend much time at the graduation.
Mom is expecting me.
I promised I wouldn't be late.

# The New Copper Penny

Some stories remain with us, embedded in our hearts, emblazoned on our souls. I refer to them as ghosts, a memory that follows us through time.
When I was much younger I heard a story about a young man who lived in my grandmother's neighborhood.
Even though he was old enough to be a man, his brain was wired differently, and he remained a boy.
He was always happy and laughed easily, a joy to everyone.
He loved life and all he came in contact with. His parents seemed richer for having him.
That he brought sweetness into their lives was not a secret. He was a gift to all in the neighborhood.

One day he was given a new copper penny. The young man had heard that money doesn't grow on trees.
He decided to plant the penny in the yard and prove this theory wrong.
He would help make his parents richer with the money from the tree.
He knew a great tree would grow money from the penny. He just knew.

Week after week and through the season of the cold snows, he watched and waited.
He knew his copper penny was taking root, even though he couldn't see it.
Spring arrived, and he watched as all the young leaves came to life around the neighborhood.
He noticed young, tender buds growing fuller, beginning to blossom.
He would rush back to his garden to see if anything had grown from his copper penny.
Every day he stayed hopeful, patiently waiting until his mother called him for dinner.
One morning he again went to see if anything had grown and was surprised.
There were tiny green shoots all over the ground where he had planted his copper penny.

He was so excited that he ran to his mother and pulled her to the garden to show her, explaining in his excited words of his plan to make them rich.
His mother did not know what to say, so she just smiled at her son.
Later that night, after dinner, she told her husband in hushed tones about their son's plans.
They both wondered what they would say to their son when a tree did not grow.
The little green shoots soon grew into colorful flowers.
Great displays of purple and yellow blossoms sprung up all around the yard.  Also tiny white flowers thickly covered the ground, like a beautiful quilt.
The young man wondered when the tree would grow, so he continued to wish for the day he could make his parents rich.
The next Saturday his father and mother came and stood beside their son.
His father told his son he knew of the gift the son wanted to give them. He explained to his son how wealthy they were already—that having him for a son made them richer than anyone they knew, that the wisdom of the tree knew there were others who needed the money more.
The young man listened to the words.
Finally his face broke into a grin.
Smiling, he said it was good the tree was so wise.
The young man was happy he had made them rich after all.
When he spotted any new trees in the neighborhood, he knew it was his new copper penny that brought riches to someone who needed it.
So the story goes.

# The Newsboy

It had been a long day, and all I wanted was to go home, shower, and read something, I thought. I looked to my right before unlocking the door of my car. A young boy I'd never seen before was selling newspapers.
Interesting, I thought. I had walked by there every day for years. He probably just started selling paper in the neighborhood.
"Hi. Nobody around to buy your papers?" I asked him.
"No, ma'am, just waiting for you, I guess," he answered, looking awkward.
"Are you always here? I don't remember seeing you before."
"I'm always somewhere close by, ma'am. Buy a paper?" he asked.
"Love to. It's been a while since I read a daily paper."
I paid him the fifty cents and turned to walk back to the car, happy about the evening that was taking shape.

A hot shower followed by a relaxed read was in the works.
I waved, and he waved back at me.
Odd, I thought, never seeing him around.
After the shower and in my pj's, I unfolded the paper and began scanning.
Then I noticed the date. It was dated a year from now.
How could that be? Must be a misprint.
The newspaper was probably receiving calls from hundreds of people.
Oh well, I thought. No biggie. Then, as I started reading, none of the news made any sense.

***A NEW WORLD COUNCIL CREATED.***
***FIRST MEETING IS SCHEDULED***
***One hundred of the world's brightest young people ages 9-17, chosen to save the planet.***

I continued reading this fantastic article and goosebumps prickled throughout my body. The paper reported that an interplanetary League of Beings had been watching Earth develop for a millennium.
I read on:
Non-interference was its primary intent; however, the planet would

reach catastrophic levels in fifty years.
Intervention was needed to save Earth. The interplanetary league said that Earth was a divine experiment that held great potential for evolution; that free will had never been interfered with. Decisions born out of greed, the continual abuse of living creatures, and our diminished resources were destroying us.
Earth was approaching a danger zone. All this has resulted in an interplanetary intervention on a grand scale. The league acknowledged there were countless efforts being made on Earth. Some remarkable and brilliant; however, growing unrest and disagreement had demanded the evolution of this council. This planet would reach catastrophic levels in fifty years.

The article continued, "The World Council was chosen from children and young adults around the world. They were inheriting all this. The overall intention is to correct the downward spiraling that would end in extinction. This diverse group of extraordinary children has already set out to establish stopgaps and cooperative partnership between all nations. As galactic proteges, these young people generate a unique energy. There would also be ten adults chosen from different businesses and governments around this world as well, including two world leaders; two environmental scientists educated in global matters of reforesting the planet, new energy production, and ocean rehabilitation; and three world-renowned health specialists with true vision and imagination behind them..." The list went on.
I sat wondering where this had all come from.
I also thought, "Wouldn't this just be wonderful." I hoped it was indeed true.
I knew I would be looking for the newsboy the next day.

# From the Heart

# Beginnings Steps

This was it. I could see this was the moment.
I said, “Yes. Go ahead. No fear!”
I listened to her respond in her way.
A faintly imperious look always presents during a challenge.
I don’t always understand her words, but the answer was clear from her lively body language.
“Yes, you can do this," I told her. “Yes, anyway, you want to,” I replied to her questioning eyes.
I kept saying yes to all her quick babbling remarks.

“Will I be good enough?” she seemed to ask.
“Yes!”
“Will they take me seriously?” I heard her ask.
“Yes.”
“I am scared!” she cried out in her way. “Will I be able to stand on my own? To face my fear?” she seemed to ask, staring into my eyes.
I said, “Yes, no, maybe, but you will have done your best.”
“What happens if no one likes me? If they laugh?”
“But most will love your courage. You can never fail,” I answered.
“There will always be a small few who will never support you,” I thought.

I watched her reach out her hand to mine.
My baby girl then took her first step toward me.
"Yes, there will always be those few, but so many others will pick you up."

# Letters Unopened

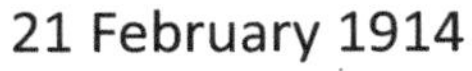

21 February 1914
Dear John,
I am wondering how you are. I have not received a letter from you in several weeks, my dear. I walk our home and land so often that I must know every nook and cranny that exists.
Robert is working the land diligently. I do not want you to feel any concern during your stay overseas.
Do well in your business, and please know all is well here.
I miss you very much, my husband.

Your loving wife, Amy

12 May 1914

Dear John,
Sweetheart, can your life be so busy that there is no word to share with me? I long for any word from you.
I lie awake for long hours at night, fearful that you have found the arms of another to hold you and whisper secrets. Please, my dearest, just a simple letter. I know it takes so long to travel across the seas. Are you still in Alsace? My greatest hope is that one day soon I will be blessed with a full packet of your letters. I can only imagine what they might say to me from your heart.

Your dearest wife

30 June 1914

Dearest,
I have news that there is a great deal of disturbance in France and Germany.
I wonder where you are, John. How you are? Are you safe? Are you still in France?
I am worried and miss you beyond anything imaginable. In the early morning the other day, I took a walk.
The wind was blowing softly on my body. I unfastened some buttons

on my blouse.
The air stirred me; the wind grew stronger. I must confess it was exhilarating. No one was at work yet. I went down to our river and walked up to the edge.
I felt so lonely for you. The water was soft and flowing slowly. I walked in farther. I was not afraid. As you know, I could never swim.
I have a secret to tell you, John. I have been going to our neighbors and learning to swim with their children. "What a lark," you may say.
I smile thinking of this first memory, sharing this experience with the Wilson children.
As I walked into the river that day, the water was up to my waist.
The feeling of it rushing through my legs and thighs was breathtaking.
I felt quite giddy. I miss you so very much.

Please let me know all is well with you, that you will come home soon.
I love you John,
Amy

*NY Herald*
*July 31, 1914*

*French Socialist leader Jean Jaures, who stood for peace during mounting battles, has been murdered. Along with Jaures were many who supported him, including Dr. John Goshen, who had acted as a liaison with the German peace movement, has also died.*

Twelve days after Amy read the news, a postal supervisor visited her. He handed her a thick packet of stained letters her husband had written to her over the previous months.

# Snow Angels

I woke up lonely, feeling on the verge of depression. It was welling up again.
It had just snowed two feet. I needed to get out of my house; it was feeling like a prison.
Bundled up, I began a walk that was about to become a very unexpected getaway. Along my walk I trudged through paths that needed to be shoveled, paths thick with dazzling new snow.
Looking around me, in awe of the quiet, I felt a sense of well-being sneaking its way into my soul.
I came upon a sizable hill. It was still untouched by footprints. Off to my left, lying in the snow under a tree, was a young girl. She was moving her arms and feet in unison. She stopped and smiled up at me. I just looked at her. What was she doing out there alone? No one else was around, anywhere.
“Hi, my name is Mary," she said and then giggled. “What’s your name?”
“Ed,” I answered.

“Are you going to make a snow angel?” she asked me.
“I never have,” I answered.

“Come on. I’ll show you how.”
I walked to her, making new footprints in the snow. After sitting down and falling backwards, I moved like she did, but I was not getting the arm-leg coordination very well, not in rhythm when I danced either.

“Do what I do and copy me. Don’t worry, Ed; there is no wrong way.”
I loosened up and just moved like a slow jumping jack, except I was lying in snow.
“Bring her to life, Ed. Just pretend.”

My eyes closed. I imagined it. A rush of laughter came up from inside me. I felt a little nuts moving my arms and legs in the snow. No one else was around.

How long I lay there making the snow angel, I don't know. I was

outrageously proud of my first snow angel. Smiling, I opened my eyes to share my accomplishment with Mary.
She wasn't there. I stood up to find her. I found only my footprints in the snow. Where were Mary's?
In the utter quiet were both our snow angels, side by side.

A sense of wonderment came over me. I will never forget this day, I thought.
I looked for her again. Mary was gone, but her snow angel remained.
I knew something unique had happened to me that day.

# Thanksgiving

To begin with, I wasn't sure how I was going to pull off Thanksgiving this year or anything that was gay and focused on being up and happy, let alone Thanksgiving.
Everything I did or said seemed forced.
There was such unhappiness in my family.
Nothing seemed real.
What was real was I wanted to scream and crawl into my husband's arms with our children.
I wanted to wake up and realize this was a bad dream, continuing to wonder about the word forever. Will this be life forever?
Looking out the bedroom window, I imagined a messenger floating down and giving him, us, another chance.
I said a prayer asking for help.
My husband, Geoff, had been hurt badly. He wouldn't be out of the hospital for weeks.
The kids were like walking shadows. The doctors told me he might never regain his memory.
This I refused to believe; however, they told me he was going to live.
"How?" I wondered.
His scratched face was yellow with added shades of horrid blue. He just lay on a pillow in this unfamiliar room surrounded by cries of sickness.
The few times I brought the kids to visit, he didn't know any of us.
During the times he opened his eyes, there was total blankness, a complete lack of understanding, no connection to anyone, anything, or even who he was. Just one of those unfortunate things, I was told by the police and everyone.
Wrong place at the wrong time.
Today was Thanksgiving.
The kids and I brought in his favorite dishes. Some small measure of joy for all of us to plan and cook.
We brought acorn squash loaded with butter and sprinkled with roasted garlic.
Of course, his favorite cranberry sauce, bright and tart, as he liked it.
Stuffing made with oysters; thick, sweet Italian sausage; and onions simmered for hours in turkey broth.

We walked into the room.
Already three weeks had passed.
I felt ripped apart, especially seeing the faces of our children.
Our two wonderfully tough children wished they were anywhere but here.
Geoff was alive. Their dad was still here.
We walked over to him. He turned and looked at me. He looked at our children.
I said, "Geoff?"
He answered me, "Diane?"
There was a long moment of feeling suspended, then tears, smiles, and kisses.
The doctor was speaking to me. I couldn't hear him.

Thanksgiving that year was a mixture of emotional well-wishers and hugs from everyone.
I stepped outside for a minute, speaking to the Universe of my gratefulness, giving thanks for this miracle.

# The Art Class

I was going to paint a portrait. The model sitting before me was lovely. Though not tall, the model was willowy in her posture. Graceful. She looked like alabaster, maybe even solid ivory. She was so still, so majestic her modeling expertise would never be doubted.
Her classical features touched a deep memory.
My mind held a partial picture.
It became more vivid as I flipped through my memory files.
I was just a beginner in painting but not in memory flipping. Déjà vu has been a companion for years.
I continued mixing my colors to see what worked, my inner picture becoming sharper.
Then I found the mental file, and I saw what became very clear. It was my maternal grandmother's face.
Her skin was beautiful, radiant.
She had been regal, a striking snow queen from Norway.
Much of the time her cheeks were rosy from being outside in her garden, which was how she spent most of her days, morning until dusk. Her sharp blue Nordic eyes searched for crawling invaders in her realm.
I observed the scenes unfolding in my mind's eye. I began writing it down on my watercolor pad.
The pictures moving through my mind came fast. My pen could barely keep up.
Then I remembered something; I was in a room shrouded in white sheets covering furniture and watching the dust particles perform a ballet in the streaming moonlight. I was witnessing a much younger self sneak into the room of shadows while the house was asleep. Remembering this time was shortly after my grandfather's death, the lifelessness of mourning still breathing all over the house.
Moonlight shining throughout the clear, vast windows that fronted my grandparents' house, stunningly intense. It was peaceful, dream-like, not like the overactive, volatile days spent with my parents.
I have come to love that younger me more through the years, realizing I had just received a gift from this memory.
Mixing my colors again, I felt Invigorated by the moments spent with this place in time.
Humming, I began painting the model but with a story now filling in the background.

# The Cleanup Crew

I was part of a cleanup crew.
My job was to clean up districts destroyed by storms.
This last one that swept through was a greedy monster wanting to take everything in its path.
It did.

It is now several months after that hurricane, one of the worst of the century, swept the East Coast. The land will never be the same, but nothing ever remains the same, anyway. I was soon to understand this more deeply.
The realization has differed in how I live my life now.
Every day is a treasure.
I volunteered for the cleanup crew in neighborhoods that were both near and far.
Some areas were hit more mildly.
Some were entirely wiped out.
The degrees of devastation were unbelievable.
I found possessions, furniture, books, appliances, and even money.
What touched me most were the photographs.
Many of the photos were still recognizable.
They touched my heart.
It was almost too much to bear.
Thousands of photos were posted on the internet, hoping some people would see theirs, pieces of a life they would want back. At the very least, it touched multitudes of human beings.
One has not left my mind. It has attached itself to my soul. Why this one?
It's a picture of a boy with a golden Labrador and her pups.
Where are they now?
Did they make it?
I need to believe they did.

# The Gift

She unwrapped the gift slowly, with great expectation.
Her presents were always something that had been used before. The doll or plaything given away and something new bought. She hoped this year she could have something new. Not used. Just hers to have first.
The little girl held her breath as she slowly ripped the bright holiday paper, untying the ribbon and the enormous bow, folding the paper so her parents could use it again. She felt her heart would break if the gift weren't what she had wished for.
If it wasn't, she would try not to show her feelings and hurt her mom.
Her gift was waiting to be discovered.
She knew things were changing, getting better. Mom smiled more.

The little girl opened the box.
Her gift was looking right at her. It was what she'd wished for.
It was the loveliest doll she'd ever seen. There weren't many dolls of color she had liked.
The eyes were golden, so alive! She hugged the doll close to her tiny chest.
"Thank you," she whispered and breathed a sigh.

# The Janitor

Leon Jimenez, the janitor, went in for another night session of sweeping, dusting, emptying the garbage, and praying.
Leon had been doing this work for thirty-five years. He had driven far to clean many places.
Ten years ago, he realized this was all there was to his life, to work in this school, to be in a school where children screamed, fought, and had little respect for the old halls.
The stories these halls could tell.
He once had dreams of becoming a famous bandleader, of going on the stage.
When his wife told him that nothing else would happen; this was their life, he became angry.
Leon had never felt like an angry man. It was a feeling he didn't like.
He was a man of the heart. A man of God, honest in everything he did.

He told God about everything. He thanked God for everything, especially for his wife. She was a good woman.
One day he took his wife on a walk through a neighborhood park. It was a lovely spring day.
He told her he was sorry he didn't make his dream come true; that he was just a janitor.
She stopped walking and took Leon in her arms.
She whispered to him that her dream had come true. It came true every morning she heard him come home and lie beside her. Every night when he left for work.
"You are the best janitor in the world, *mí amore*. I could not be prouder of who I am married to," she spoke in a soft voice.
"When you used to sing to me and play your soft guitar, I was in heaven.
"I miss those times."
Leon stepped livelier in the coming days.
He had found his dream.
Leon played his guitar again. He was a rich man indeed.

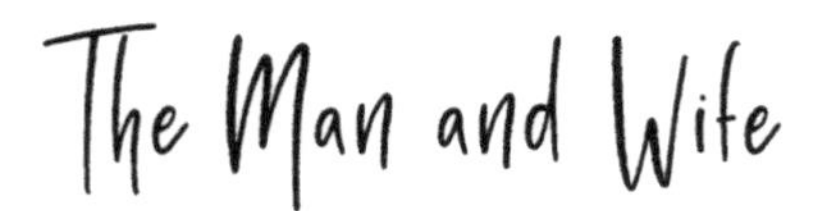

# The Man and Wife

I remember the day when I started speaking more softly to my wife.
Our life started to unravel when the doctor diagnosed her with a deteriorating condition in her brain.
She no longer grasped what was being said. I noticed she would go away somewhere in her mind, her eventual prison.
I could not reach her. It scared me because I had always loved our conversations.
As time passed I realized I could no longer reach her in the world she had entered.
I became lonely, despairing at a loss to share anything with her.

Eventually our days consisted of driving the car to the local gym.
We'd always enjoyed the drive to the gym, and it seemed to remain a connection for us.
I felt she was with me during those drives. She knew me and seemed to feel safe.
I would guide her toward the exercise bike, and as weeks passed, I walked with her on the indoor track.
After months I found two women who adopted us as a couple.
My wife seemed at ease with these women.
They understood I still hungered for conversation, to share thoughts, opinions, and ideas.
It was natural to begin a friendship with them. The four of us enjoyed our time together.
We would meet at the gym often to walk and talk. Their friendship aided me, even after my wife passed.
I later married one of the women.
Knowing she had also known my first wife was a comfort.
Did my wife sense the eventual outcome of all of this?
Perhaps; she had been a wise woman.

# The Village

Pablo waited at the top of the stairs, taking great pleasure in the pictures streaming through his mind's eye. He was steps away from opening his front door and once again finding out what nighttime looked like in his village. He opened his door and watched the people from his village, the town where he had grown up and lived his life, strolling arm and arm. It had been more than a year without the walking, talking, and laughing. Over the past year, people talked with each other only from windows and doorways since the pandemic arrived in full force. Hearing shouts of how people were doing and sharing bits of news from each household was the daily event. He had heard the raised voices of friends and loved ones buzzing every morning and evening. Sometimes songs would break out and join with other voices. Most were alive and healthy. This was life during the pandemic. This evening the vivid shades of the women's skirts and blouses lit up the night, as did the distinctive hats worn by men known only to this village. Every style of a villager's hat told a story, a story of the rains that turned torrential, washing away homes; the heat and sun blazing beyond hot but also producing the finest regional wine and tobacco.

When it seemed the disease would never end, it did. The joy and celebrations would begin this evening.

Pablo thought about all these things as he stepped onto the street. The aromas and influences of colors stopped him in his steps. He just stood watching and savoring it all. He was ready to taste the foods the street vendors would offer, beginning with free samples of their specialties. These sellers came from many provinces and had original foods and gifts from far and wide.

He listened to the music beginning, the sweet sounds of guitars and wind instruments echoing fragile, haunting sounds that would continue throughout the night. All native to this region. His village, his home.

Pablo walked down the street carrying his instrument with him.

Yes, tonight he would sing the love songs of his village while he looked for his beloved.

# Fanciful

# Meteor Humor

Crash!
"What the heck?" I rush to the back door. I don't know what to expect.
Not what I saw.
My mind and senses are spinning. Is this a dream?
Split down the middle of my old, immense oak tree is an oval-shaped disk.
The disk is about seven feet in diameter. It is humming. Tiny lights go on and off all around the green shape.
I move toward it. I stand before the pulsating orb as a panel opens up.
Long fingers reach out and hand me a sealed envelope.
I reach for it, realizing I am also vibrating. Looking at my body, I notice it is mirroring the twinkling lights. I have never felt quite so calm.
"What is this thing?" I wonder. "What is going on? Should I open the envelope?"
I open it. Inside the envelope is a letter. I read the letter. What I read is direct and clear.
"Take me to your leader."
"Really?" I wonder who to call.
I decide to go inside, light some candles, and call my mother.

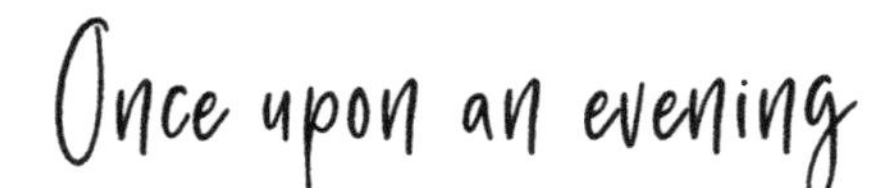

# Once upon an evening

The man had been mocking with his wisecracks, verbally abusive.
He immediately realized he had blundered.
A raven flew into the room through the window.
Long fingers moved so fast they echoed in the air.
"I take offense at that remark, sir," the witch said softly.
"Whatever," he growled under his breath.
The witch had no other recourse with his sort.
She began her chant.
The world would feel one less burden with him gone.
What was once air became fluid as the witch directed her energy.
As the man receded into a sleeplike state, there was a long sigh heard.
Footsteps could be heard leaving.
There was nothing to be seen anymore where the man had stood.

*Hell has no fury*
*as a witch, that has been scorned.*
*Beware the payback.*

She stirred slowly from her bed to stand up, her eyes still sleepy with dream sand.
She began to focus.
The young woman wondered if the powers would visit her today.
It had been a long, intense shift last night.
She took a deep breath, closed her eyes, and swung her arms in an arc.
It would be a great time to receive the powers after such a demanding night.
Opening her eyes, she felt the force. Her power was alive!
Moving to a larger space in her apartment, she opened her arms wide to receive.
Pausing, she took a breath, held it, and blew it out with a powerful *whoosh*.
Yes, the Force was with her.
About to twirl, she remembered the last time she did. She almost took out half her room, knocking over a lamp, toppling a plant, nearly breaking a window with the energy that surged.
On her dresser lay her headdress of purple and pink feathers laced with gold streamers.
Her cloak of satin and leather hung on a hook, the colors blending with her headdress.
“After all,” she thought, “in the everyday world, why not look your best?”
Deep golds woven in the black velvet and rich fuchsia adorned her cloak.
The tail she often imagined at the base of her spine was there, full, fluffy, and thick.
She envisioned holding it.
Stroking the tail, she could see the glee on the children’s faces tonight.
She would wear her headdress and cloak on her shift tonight.
Tonight she would share her imagined tail with her children.
The children in the ICU would enjoy this.
She would make sure they all had their own tails by her shift’s end.

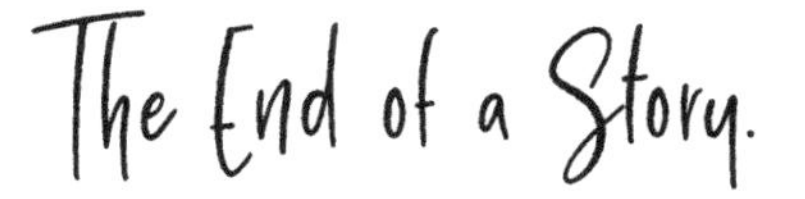

# The End of a Story.

The book had been a major part of Anna's life for the last thirty days. She was depressed knowing there was only one final, brief chapter remaining, and then the inescapable last page.
It had been a fabulous month. The book wove its way into every part of her days. Questions flooded her mind about the ending.
She had thought of several endings. How would the author end it?

Anna lay in bed thinking about all of the possibilities.
Her bed pillows had been fluffed and the room scented with lavender, all in readiness for the last chapter. She felt very edgy.
The unknown ending will surely bring forth a torrent of tears or smiles. This book had done it all along.
She had lived it. She had loved it. The way the story wove together the words had moved her profoundly.
They stayed with her. They had taken root.
After reading the final chapter, Anna turned to the last page. The clock in her room ticked away the minutes. A lonely tear trailed down Anna's cheek.
She kept reading, and then she smiled.

# The Night Shift

In silent numbers they drag themselves to pubs known to only a few, the crews that work the odd hours: the hours when most of us are asleep, counting sheep, safe in our beds, not mindful of the others who unload cargo that any sensible mind wouldn't approach.
Some pubs stay open for these men of anonymity. They ache for rest after long nights in the empires of metal, machines, and massive trunks of lumber.
Sweating bodies lifted cargo from the hulls of the ships. Ships arrived from countries too distant and mysterious to think about, names too complicated to pronounce. The languages spoken differently from their own.
The deep bellies of these beasts that sail the seas birthed their load with the help of these men under the secrecy of night.
Night after night these men gather, braced for twelve hours of what is expected of them. No more, no less, union leaders ever watching.
When the shift is over, released for a time, they enter the pubs and order a drink and a meal. The best carved meat; potatoes; and soft, thick slices of white bread right out of the ovens all washed down with a beer and a shot. Mana from some heaven before bed.
There are also the women who stand by to offer for a small price some temporary solace from the agony of the shift.
These full-breasted women understand the men, tempting them with bodies ready to offer comfort.
Only the darkened corners of the pub know. It is a secret kept.
As daylight nears, the hours of laughing and camaraderie end.
The agony of crushed fingers and bones surface.
With backs strained beyond recovery, the workers pull their caps lower and head home, to a bed, to another loving body with open arms.
Home to sleep but not to dream, for night comes soon.
The pub will be ready, ready for the men of the midnight shift and the dollars exchanged from broken hands, the faces filled with laughter and tears from another night shift.

# The Sheriff of Iron Bark Court

I heard the chattering, shucking, and tsking. I knew the guardian of my yard was on high alert.
By then I regarded the squirrel as the sheriff.
A big gray-and-white cat sat under a leafless tree in my backyard.
Even though the leaves were gone, the cat must have felt cloaked.
Undercover, the tabby just sat and waited.
The sheriff, as big and fluffy as the cat, chattered on in raucous sounds that built to an incredible volume. I believed the squirrel was alerting a family of chipmunks to be wary.
The chipmunk family, I had learned, lived under my patio.

"The cat is here!" the sheriff screamed in distinctive tones.
I shooed the cat away, telling it to go home, cursing the owners of the cat. I returned to what I was doing.
Later that afternoon, I heard another sound. The sound drew me once again to look. I saw fallen leaves swirling in my backyard.
Play was in full force.
The squirrel was chasing a friend around. They were playing tag.
Smaller than the sheriff, the chipmunks were bathing in the warming sun.
They had babies. They were so tiny. I watched them peek around at this new world of theirs.
All was well with the world. The sheriff was on the job.

# The Wild Woman and the Teddy Bear

As the story goes, she was coming back from her walk through the forest.
Her feet were toughened by the many surfaces she had walked on throughout the years.
Some were spongy moss beds, others hot and hard.
At times the ground was so dry and cracked it appeared lifeless, but it was not true.
The woman always saw aliveness wherever she was.
She had satisfied her thirst with water throughout the day. Now she was looking forward to a glass of excellent local red wine.
Her walk continued toward her temporary home in this cozy retreat.
Images of soaking in a scented bubble bath quickened her steps.
The moon had risen recently, and she had howled in honor of her animal within, a ritual she had learned long ago, to give thanks, grateful for being alive.
The woman bayed mindfully, so as not to bring any attention to the personal moment between her and Grandmother Moon.
This evening she had felt the rhythm moving, inviting her to dance.
Her body swirled, almost primal in the movements.
She felt her feet skip and stamp the earth, grounding her in her dance of gratefulness to Mother Gaia, to divine Universe.
But for all that, the story I am sharing is a kind of love story.
A unique love story.

Continuing her walk back, she spotted a bundle on the ground in the bright moonlight.
The woman picked it up.
It was a teddy bear.
Looking at it, she saw it had been in the forest for a while.
She brought it tenderly to her breast and kept walking toward her destination.
The forest she was in was a cork forest in Portugal.
One promise to herself was to travel to many forests and woods throughout the world.
Some were well known and some not.
After opening the door to her room, she put her precious bundle on

the small bar. She looked at the little eyes of the teddy bear. The eyes seemed alive.
There was no doubt someone had dropped the little stuffed animal. Some child?

The bear's eyes spoke to the woman of affection, love, and loneliness. It had been several years since her pets had passed. The pain still echoed deep within her.
She carried the little bear to the couch, once again holding it to her chest.
"Silly," she thought. But believe it or don't, as you hear this story, a feeling of protective love opened in the woman's heart.

To this day, she has shared with me that bear always travels with her. She often laughs and says, "It was a gift from the night she had howled at the moon in the cork forest."
I look at stuffed animals differently now, wondering at the feelings they can evoke.
Are these feelings exchangeable?
In the woman's case, there is not a doubt in my mind.

# Acknowledgments

*To all my friends who have listened to my plans (which sometimes change weekly), over and over; thank you for your patience and encouragement.*
*I always feel you have my back. You are the wind beneath my wings.*

*To my husband, Ron, who never fails to be a friend. He enters into my imagination of creative projects with enthusiasm and belief in me.*

*Howard Rice, teacher, professor, and wise man, once again I am grateful to you for consistently showing me what can be created in ten minutes of writing.*
*You are an awesome and an amazing soul!*

*Thank the many artists and photographers that work with copyright-free websites. You make it easy for people like me to search for the perfect image. Until it just shows up, I am quite mad. Many of these stories evoked an imagined picture of something I needed to create. These are blends of my photos and other images as well.*

*Jessica Reilley, who is my right hand, is always assisting me to recreate myself and my website. She has been with me through years of professional changes and my endless places of curiosity.*
*I thank the stars for finding A Mix of Pixels.*

*To Nathan Barker English: You saved me from pulling out my hair with redoing many images. For this I will remember you.*

*To everyone who assisted me at Outskirts Press, "Salut!"*

*Many people have inspired me, touched me in ways that took root years ago and every new day.*
*Thank you with all my soul and heart.*

*To the sun, moon, stars, and every living creature that wondrously shares in it all.*

# About CK Sobey

*CK (Kas) Sobey continues to live a life of curiosity. She considers herself to be a seeker, an explorer.*
*Her many ventures in life attest to this fact. In her earlier years she studied singing and theater. Kas is a trained mediator and worked in the San Diego dispute resolution department.*
*She also worked in the corporate world for almost thirty years.*
*Practicing as a spiritual practitioner she later became a certified hypnotherapist, bringing a deeper understanding of the inner mind to others.*
*She has facilitated groups in a variety of subjects and SoulCollage® for years.*
*Kas has since retired from her businesses to spend more time reimagining her life.*
*She enjoys cooking, walking, dancing, photography, and exploring new ideas.*
*Bubble baths with a mixture of music are her ways of unwinding at the end of a day.*
*For the past twenty years, Kas has lived in the Valley Forge area of Pennsylvania doing her best to listen to what is calling her.*
*You can often find her on new paths and retracing some older ones with a different lens.*
*When CK (Kas) is not writing or in her studio creating something that has caught her attention, she can be found in her kitchen cooking and savoring a dish with a blend of aromas wafting about or somewhere on one of her trails, waving.*
*She is also the author of a young children's book; Henry the Turtle, and book of poetic prose and photography; Musings, Woolgathering, & Ghosts.*

## *Diminutive Tales from the Tip of My Imagination*

A few muses hang around me most days. Sometimes it feels like a rabbit that hops along, inviting me to follow. Down that proverbial rabbit hole. It is a process that I trust, at least to begin. If I am in the flow, the zone, it leads to the next step.
The creative spirit is unique in what she offers us. It begins with receiving. It never ceases to amaze me. This spirit is always waiting to be realized. There are no boundaries. Creativity can be spontaneous.

## From *A Collection of Tiny Stories*

A Collection of Tiny Stories: Diminutive Tales from the Tip of My Imagination *presents prose and art that represent an inspirational celebration of the spirit, gathering "tiny" works "born out of moments of whimsy, mystery, and longing." Add "and magic" to that list, because CK Sobey's works employ a magical element that gather tales both fantastic and reflective into three sections:* Inspiring Odysseys, From the Heart, *and* Fanciful.

*These short works don't require linear reading. Readers can skip through the sections and will find them succinct, standalone pieces that delight no matter their arrangement or the wellsprings of their wonder.*

*Take "The Bookstore" for one example. Here, Sobey reflects* "I always love going to the bookstore. I go when I'm drained, or my inner animal needs its fur stroked." *The piece goes on to explore the magic of a particular used book that calls his name with intrigue to provide passages that fuel his days:* "I knew we would eventually meet." It was handwritten in a beautiful, fluid script. Intrigue and enchantment came over me. I touched those written words with my fingers, stroking the words."

D. Donovan, Sr., Reviewer,
Midwest Book Review

*CK Sobey brings tiny stories that open big doors of imagination and send us sparks to ignite our own creative fires. These stories cover a gamut of life experiences, including wonder, curiosity, illness and death, tenderheartedness, and laughter. The weaving in of images provides visual inspiration that makes this collection even more delightful.*

Gail Warner, MA, MFT,
author of *Weaving Myself Awake: Voicing the Sacred through Poetry,*
therapist, and founder of Pine Manor Retreat Center.

"The magic is coming back" *says the typewriter... Kassia reminds us that it has never left the crevices between moments and invites us to look. These stories are like wild strawberries found while we are walking in the woods on a hot day. You will savor, you will giggle, you will wonder, and sometimes you might shed a tear. The beautifully curated images are poems in themselves. Lose yourself in them and use them as portals to your own imagination.*

Mariabruna Sirabella, MS, LMFT, SCF&T
*www.mariabruna.com*
Founder of the School Of The Origins
SoulCollage® Lead Trainer; Trainings and Translations Coordinator

CPSIA information can be obtained
at www.ICGtesting.com
Printed in the USA
LVHW071026190622
721603LV00010B/488